This Little Tiger book belongs to:

_____

_____

_____

_____

For Carl ~ C F

For Sarah, Chris and Hannah ~ S M

LITTLE TIGER PRESS
An imprint of Magi Publications
1 The Coda Centre, 189 Munster Road, London SW6 6AW
www.littletigerpress.com

First published in Great Britain 2007

Text copyright © Claire Freedman 2007
Illustrations copyright © Simon Mendez 2007
Claire Freedman and Simon Mendez have asserted their rights
to be identified as the author and illustrator of this work under
the Copyright, Designs and Patents Act, 1988

A CIP catalogue record for this book is available
from the British Library

Printed in China

2 4 6 8 10 9 7 5 3 1

I Love You, Sleepyhead

Claire Freedman Simon Mendez

LITTLE TIGER PRESS
London

Look, little child,
as the night is unfurled,
Animals going to bed
round the world.

Close to her mother,
safe by her side,
Sweet little fawn
is so sleepy-eyed.

Nestled in grass,
as the soft breezes blow,
Bathed by the warmth
of the sun's evening glow.

Lion cubs romp as the sun slips away.
In the soft golden light, there's still time to play.

Soon they'll be yawning, three tired sleepyheads,
Watched by their mother all night in their beds.

Waddling to Mummy,
the tired ducklings quack,
Sleepy from swimming,
they're glad to be back.

Safely they're tucked
in their nest for the night,
Feathery bundles,
huddled up tight.

Daylight is fading fast, softly dusk falls.
"Bedtime now, little ones," mother fox calls.

"Mum, we're not sleepy!" the small foxes cry,
As low in the pale sky, the sun says goodbye.

Wrapped up in love,
little bear feels so snug,
Cuddled goodnight
in a big mummy-hug.

Drifting to sleep
he sinks into her fur,
Warm in the soft snow,
snuggled with her.

High up, the trees catch the last rays of sun,
As three tired monkeys climb up to their mum.

The sounds of the jungle, the rustling leaves,
Lull them to sleep in the cool evening breeze.

Snug with their mummy,
the rabbits are all
Tumbled together
in one furry ball.

Cosy and warm,
they will sleep safe and sound,
Curled in their bed
on the soft mossy ground.

Rocked by the waves
beneath velvet blue skies,
Wrapped in her mummy's arms,
small otter lies.

Under the stars
in the dappled moonlight,
"One kiss," smiles Mummy,
"and then it's sleep-tight."

Snowflakes are swirling,
all fluffy and white,
Sparkling like stars in the
gleaming moonlight.

Cuddled up close,
little penguin stays warm,
Through the cold frosty night,
till the first light of dawn.

As mother owl hoots
her sweet, low lullaby,
Her baby owls blink
at the star-studded sky.

Through the dark treetops,
her echoing call,
Sings to the world,
"A good night to you all!"

Baby whale drifts
to the deep ocean's song,
Close to his mother,
all the night long.

Down through the water,
the soft moonlight streams,
As little whale floats
in a sea of sweet dreams.

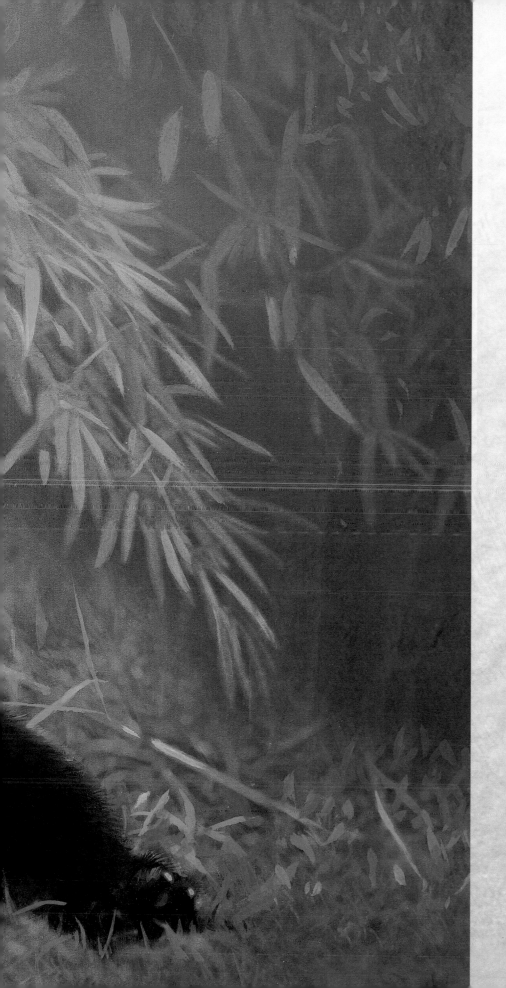

Small panda sleeps
as the stars peek-a-boo,
Held by his mother,
all the night through.

Cuddled up close,
she gives him a kiss.
Tucked up together,
they're perfect like this.

Sleep, child, like the animals,
in the starlight.
I love you, sleepyhead,
sweet dreams – goodnight!

Cuddle down to sleep with these endearing Little Tiger Press books

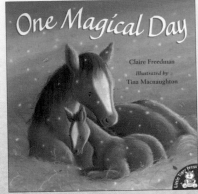

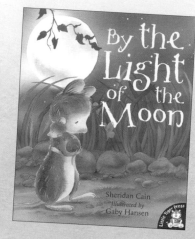

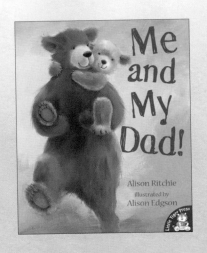

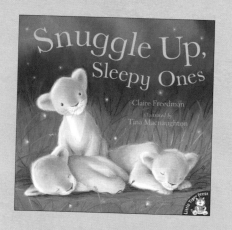

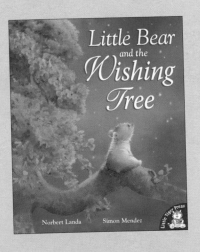

For information regarding any of the above titles
or for our catalogue, please contact us:
Little Tiger Press, 1 The Coda Centre,
189 Munster Road, London SW6 6AW
Tel: 020 7385 6333 Fax: 020 7385 7333
E-mail: info@littletiger.co.uk
www.littletigerpress.com